Kath Middleton beg ϵ
(100-word stories) ar

Jonathan Hill's second drabble collection. It wasn't long before she moved up a size to contribute short stories to anthologies. Shortly afterwards, she progressed to writing longer pieces and already she has a considerable back catalogue of acclaimed work. Kath likes to put her characters in difficult situations and watch them work their way out. She believes in the indomitable nature of the human spirit (and chickens). Kath is retired. She graduated in geology and has a certificate in archaeology. When she's in a hole, she doesn't stop digging.

ISBN-10: 1540638693
ISBN-13: 978-1540638694

www.kathmiddletonbooks.com

Stir-up Sunday: the Sunday before Advent in the Christian church's calendar; traditionally the day Christmas puddings are made, each family member stirring and making a wish; *(unconfirmed) a day when restless spirits make themselves known*

Then

LIZZY SANG as she worked. It was tiring but nobody working on a farm expected a light job. She'd rather be a dairymaid than work outside like the farmhands did. That was punishing in cold weather like this. She could see her breath as a cloud in the air, and her reddened hands were often chapped and raw after a day separating the cream, making butter or cheese, or simply moving the big churns around.

She was used to the cold, of course. The dairy was always chilly, even on a hot summer's day, let alone an icy, late-November morning like this. The flooring was stone slabs over packed earth and the room faced north. Anything to keep the milk cool. Pushing back a lock of hair with her wrist, she carried on stirring the sticky mixture in the flickering pre-dawn candlelight.

Today was a special day – a once-a-year day. Lizzy had been up extra-early to make the Christmas puddings. It took all day to boil them in the huge pans so she had to get the mixture ready in good time. Stir-up Sunday, they called it. The day you made the puddings. Mrs Caldwell, Farmer's missus, would be in shortly to stir the ingredients and make a wish. Then her two children would take a turn, and any of the other farm workers who chose to. It made her proud to be the one making the pudding when everyone got their wish from it. At least, she hoped they did. It was important in wish-making that you never told a soul what you'd wished for.

Lizzy loved the smell associated with this task. It would be her third year making the puddings. Missus had shown her how the first time, and now it was all her job. She loved the sweet aromas of the dark sugar and the spices, the sourness of the stout, and the sharpness of the lemon juice and zest. There were all the fruits to be cleaned and soaked in Farmer's special brandy the night before. Flour and breadcrumbs just enough to hold it all together, eggs from the chickens that scratched in the daytime outside the dairy door and a handful of chopped nuts to give it some texture. The whole came together as a speckled, scented mystery. It was like magic, or maybe alchemy.

She heard the outer door sneck clatter behind her. That'd be Roy coming in with the first churn full of milk. Once she'd put the puddings into the floured clouts and Missus had lowered them into the boiling water in the farmhouse kitchen, she'd be back making the cheese and the butter as usual. No rest for the wicked, they say.

"How do, Roy? Just put it over there out of my way, will you, love? I'll get to it in a minute."

There was no cheery greeting or reply. Strange. She knew Roy was sweet on her. He usually came in all chatty of a morning, but sometimes he'd hang about afterwards, looking flustered and abashed. In fact, she'd thought of making him the subject of her secret wish. But he wasn't usually so reticent. Pausing in the mixing, she half-turned towards the outer door. It was just getting light and a shadowy figure stood with the pink dawn behind him, almost blocking the doorway.

"Oh, it's you, Edgar. Don't leave the door open. It's perishing in here."

The door hit the frame as Edgar Burton, the farm's visiting farrier, entered and walked up behind her. She turned to resume her work.

"What do you want in here? I'm that busy, what with the puddings and all. It's Stir-up Sunday and Missus will have the big pots on to boil. I've got to get on."

Still he said nothing. By rights, he shouldn't be in the dairy. He ought to have been over in the stables, though the horses would be out by now. Sunday morning it may be but the work never stopped. Half a day on Saturday and every third Sunday was her usual time off. "Does Farmer know you're here?" she asked, continuing with her work. "Which horse have you come for? Only I got to get on with this."

She felt a sudden alarm. She could feel, in the chilly place, a hot breath on her neck.

"Don't act cute wi' me, Lizzy Pelham," the farrier's rough voice assaulted her ear. "You know what I've come here for."

"I most certainly don't and you can keep your

hands to yourself or I'll call for the lads."

"They're all over in Top Field. There's nobody to hear you here."

He pressed into her from behind, so she couldn't turn. His rough whiskers scraped the nape of her neck where her hair was tied up and out of the way.

"How dare you?" she cried, beating at the air behind her with the huge wooden mixing paddle. She heard his nasty laugh. The coward. He'd waited till everyone was away, busy elsewhere on the farm, to try to force her.

"You know you want it. I've seen the way you look at the lads. You're ripe for picking and nobody else is man enough to do it round here. Come on, stir yourself, Lizzy," he muttered in a choked voice as he pushed her skirts up around her waist.

She screamed, flailing about her with the sticky, wooden paddle and knocking the guttering candle. It rolled in a circle before hitting the flagstones, increasing the dimness of the dairy. She screamed again. Wouldn't someone hear her and come?

Now

"CAN I MAKE the Christmas puddings this year, Mum? It's going to be my last Christmas at home."

"For goodness' sake, Hannah! You're only getting a flat a couple of miles away. You're not off to Australia, you know. You'll be back here every week for your Sunday dinners if I'm not much mistaken. And what was stopping you before? You can mix the puddings any time you like."

"I know but I never particularly wanted to before. It's all that watching Bake-Off!"

Hannah's mum laughed as she continued writing the shopping list for the extra ingredients she'd need. "Of course you can. I'll get all the stuff in ready and you can make them. Use my old recipe book, the handwritten one. It's the book your great-gran started. That's the best pudding recipe I've ever tasted."

"I know. The family Christmas Pud recipe, all in that spidery handwriting. And everyone seems to have added their own recipes to that book since."

"We have. It'll be passed down to you eventually. But I always use the traditional family pudding recipe from there. I tried a couple from cookery books years ago but they were never as good. You need to do them tomorrow morning, you know. Stir-up Sunday, it's called."

Liam, Hannah's seventeen year old brother, dashed in at that point looking for his mobile phone. "What on earth's Stir-up Sunday?" he asked with one of his twisted half-smiles.

"Don't pull that expression, dear. It makes you look like a gangster," his mum said.

"Well, I know Gran used to let us all have a go..."

"Three stirs and a wish, she always said," Hannah interrupted.

"Yeah, well, whatever..."

"It's not to do with that, really," said Mum. "It's the Collect of the last Sunday of the church's year. If you went to the village church tomorrow morning, you'd hear it at the beginning of the service." From the look on Liam's face that wasn't going to happen. She quoted, "Stir up, we beseech thee, O Lord, the wills of thy faithful people... and so on."

"Anyway, it's a tradition to make it on that day," said Hannah, "so that's when I'm going to do it!"

She went with her mum later that morning to buy the extras. These were the things they didn't usually have in the farmhouse kitchen. They always had flour and raisins and although they could raid the drinks cupboard for some brandy, Dad didn't drink stout so they had to buy a can of that. And some suet. Again, not something her mum generally kept in stock.

Mum had also checked out the spices before they went out. "They lose their flavour if you keep them too long," she'd said. They bought new ground cloves and more nutmeg, but the mixed spice was recent as her mum used it regularly in fruit cakes.

They came back in and unpacked all the ingredients which were soon swallowed up into the farmhouse kitchen's many capacious cupboards.

"I'd get all the ingredients prepared this evening

if I were you," her mum suggested. "Then you just have to mix it all up on Sunday and start the steaming. It'll need eight hours. This amount will make two good-sized puddings so we'll eat one on the day and save one for Easter, like I usually do. You can't just walk out on it either," she added. "You need to keep an eye on the water level in the pans. When it goes down a bit, top it up from the kettle – keep it all boiling. I usually set the timer to go off every couple of hours. Burning Christmas pudding is a terrible smell. You only do it once."

"Why don't you make them today?" asked Liam. "We've been invited to go to the pictures with Aunty Jo and the lads tomorrow afternoon. You'll have to miss it if you're a slave to the timer and the kettle. Or make them on Monday?"

"Don't you let your gran hear you saying that, our Liam," his mum said. "She'll give you a right earful."

"What about?"

"The time she tried to make it the week before because they were so busy. She never quite says what the problem was but she keeps saying things like, 'It was dreadful,' and 'I'd never try doing that again.'"

"Yeah, but she's old and a bit daft, isn't she?"

"Liam Clark! Don't ever let me hear you saying that about your gran again!"

"Yeah, well… She says some right funny things. What can go wrong with making Christmas puddings?"

"It's not what goes wrong, Liam. It's the kitchen. The old dairy as was. She said it never felt right if she did it on a different day. Anyway, that's all speculation because we're doing it on Sunday, aren't we, Hannah?"

Hannah nodded at her mum and shrugged at her brother. She'd go with anything for a quiet life.

Then

LIZZY STOPPED SCREAMING, pushed back hard against Edgar and smacked him in the face with the back of her head.

"Oh, you little bitch!" He grabbed her and turned her to face him.

Just then they heard the voice of Mrs Caldwell approaching the dairy, which was connected to the house by a stout door. They could clearly hear her saying, "Whatever is all that row about? Are we nearly ready for the wishes, Lizzy?"

"I've not finished with you, madam!" growled Edgar as he left rapidly through the yard door.

Lizzy hurriedly straightened her dress. Her heart was beating so fiercely she felt sure it must be visible through her ruched bodice.

"Just about there, Missus," she called, trying to regain her usual bright and bouncy voice.

"I've brought Billy and Sarah along to stir the pudding too," said Mrs Caldwell as she pushed the door open. A gust of moist warmth blew in with her from the kitchen beyond, where the water was boiling in readiness. "Oh, that does smell good. It's the start of the Christmas season for me, that smell. I know that according to the church, it's nearly Advent but for those people involved in preparing, this is when it really starts. It'll be time to make the mincemeat next!"

The short, stocky woman bustled in with the younger generation. Billy was almost Lizzy's age and did a man's work on the farm. Mrs Caldwell made him go over to the old stone sink and scrub his hands before she let him touch the big mixing paddle. Sarah, still thirteen, was learning all the housewifely arts from her mother and would no doubt take over the pudding making in another two or three years. Lizzy wanted to enjoy this privilege as long as she was able.

Mrs Caldwell took the big wooden stirrer from Lizzy's hand and, closing her eyes, stirred the pudding mixture three times anticlockwise, or widdershins as Farmer would call it. "One, two, three," she counted as the big stirrer moved sluggishly through the heavy mixture. "Now you, our Billy!"

"Oh, mother! I'm not a child now, you know. I only popped back in to see if Roy was in here."

"Well now you're here, make a wish. You used to love doing it when you were a child."

"I used to do a lot of things as a child I don't do now," he complained as he took the paddle from her hand and raked it through the pudding mix. "There, will that do?"

"Did you close your eyes and make a wish?" his mother asked.

"Yes," he said, but with such a sigh that Lizzy was sure he was just keeping her sweet. "Have you seen Roy this morning?" he asked her while Sarah took her turn with the pudding, far more eagerly than her brother had.

"No. I thought I heard him coming in here a short while back but it was Edgar."

"What's Edgar doing here this morning?"

A cold fear clutched at Lizzy's heart. And where

was Roy?

"I dunno," she said. "I was expecting Roy in here with the milk churns half an hour ago. I hope nothing's... nothing's happened to him."

"Why should anything have happened to him?" asked Billy. "I'm off out again now. I'll look out for him and tell him to get that milk down here right away. Can't have dairymaids standing about idle, can we?" He gave her a wink and left by the yard door.

Mrs Caldwell brought in the big, floured pudding clouts. While Lizzy held the massive stoneware pancheon, she used the stirring paddle to divide the mixture between the two cloths. She scraped the last of it out and smiled at Lizzy.

"Job well done, Lizzy. Thank you. I'll get these into the water now while you just clean up in here. I expect the new milk will be in shortly and it's back to work again, eh?"

The farmer's wife tied the cloths at the top with string to form a ball of pudding mixture. She carried them one at a time out of the dairy and into the farmhouse kitchen to put them into the pots on the big range.

Lizzy took the pancheon over to the stone sink and half-filled it with water. She followed Mrs Caldwell into the kitchen for a jug of hot water from the kettle over the fire. If she didn't add hot water to warm it, the suet would leave a greasy residue. At least when she'd finished, her hands would be warm for the first time today.

Now

OLD MRS CLARK, Hannah's gran and Lucy Clark's mother-in-law, arrived on Saturday for her usual weekend visit. She still lived in the neighbouring village, though Granddad Clark had died three years ago. Hannah knew that Gran felt lonely now on her own and she still enjoyed the noisy family atmosphere of the farm. She was fiercely independent, though, and wouldn't give up her home. Not while she could still manage it herself. She had run Yew Tree Farm before Hannah's mum and loved to tell them about how things were done 'in her day'.

"You're still alive, Gran. It's still your day, isn't it?" Hannah said. She hoped she'd never have this kind of searing nostalgia when she got old.

"Aye, I suppose it is, but as you get older, you feel you're losing your grip on it. You wait! You'll see what I'm talking about. And your mother tells me you're making the puddings this year?"

"Yes. I'm really looking forward to it. I like baking and I've done a steamed pudding before but never anything with all this fruit and spices and stuff. They seem to take ages to cook, too."

"They do, you're right. And that's not the finish of it either. The one we have on Christmas Day will need another two hours of steaming before we eat it."

"So you used to make them, back when you married Granddad Clark?"

"I did and his mum did it before me, and all from that recipe. Mind you, back then, we used the old kitchen – this half of your kitchen. Your dad was nearly grown up when we decided to extend the room. The old dairy was disused by then. The milk was tankered away to be bottled at the big plant and the cream and butter were made off the farm too. It all got mechanised."

"Did you just have to knock the wall down between them?" Hannah asked.

"More or less, yes. The old dairy backed onto the

farm kitchen. It was handy, see, to pop in and out. Back in the day they had proper dairymaids and the cows were milked by hand too. When it all got mechanical, it weren't worth keeping the dairy on. It was just too old-fashioned. Mind you, the builders who did it, they had to bring the floor up a bit. There was a step down from the kitchen to the dairy, and we couldn't have a change of level in the new big kitchen. People'd have been tripping up it or falling down it."

"How did they manage in just half of this room when they had farmhands to feed in here as well as the family?"

"Oh, people managed. They had to. You didn't get all this fancy cooking back then. It was all basic. Just a few great big pans, a huge oven and plenty of plates and bowls, that's all you needed. You'll be mixing the pudding up tomorrow?"

"Oh, yes. Mum's told me there's not an option!"

"Well, I don't like to speak out of turn," Gran began in a lowered voice, though it looked as though she liked it a great deal, "but once, only once, mind, I decided to make them the week before. We'd a big family gathering planned for Stir-up Sunday and I thought it'd spread the load, like."

"So what happened?"

"I don't like to say," her gran said. "It scared the life out of me, I can tell you that."

"Scared you? Why? What happened?"

Her gran looked around her to check that they were alone in the kitchen. "I was over there," she said, pointing at the outer wall, where the long worktop ran. "I was in the middle of the mixing when the place went freezing cold. I had this feeling of dread, you know, like I knew something bad was about to happen. Then I heard this whispering."

"Oh, the Haunted Kitchen," said Hannah in her best melodramatic voice, then saw from the look on her grandmother's face that she'd said the wrong thing.

"You can scoff, Miss, but I'll tell you now, I didn't ever try to do it on any day but Stir-up Sunday again. And I never liked to make it over there, on that worktop, neither. I always moved over to the old part of the kitchen to make them. I can't explain it but I know what I heard and what I felt. I don't mind admitting, it scared me a bit, did that."

Then

LIZZY WAS DRYING HER HANDS on one of the rough scrim cloths when the sneck on the outer door rattled again. Her heart rose. This must be Roy. Surely he'd got the first churn filled and ready for her by now? Whoever it was, she turned to face the door. If it was that Edgar again, she'd be ready for him this time.

It was, and he came looming into the dairy with a leer. "What's up, Lizzy? Looking for your sweetheart, was you?"

She stood her ground, hands on hips and an eye on the big metal skimmer which rested on the scrubbed wooden draining board by the sink. "What are you doing back here? If you're after the same as last time you can clear off. If you touch me I'll fight back and I'll scream the place down."

"Try it, lovely. Nobody will hear you. You just

got lucky last time."

"Missus will hear me. She's only through in the kitchen with the puddings."

"She ain't, you know. She and Sarah's upstairs making the beds. I checked. I'm not the fool you think I am, Miss High and Mighty Pelham."

"Roy will hear me, then. He'll only be across the yard in the milking shed."

The leer spread across Edgar's face like a crack in stone. "Oh no, he won't hear you. I've made sure o' that."

"What have you done to him? You've not hurt him, have you? There'll be no more work here for you if Farmer finds out you've hurt one of his workers. Can't you see that? Are you that blinded with it?"

"Blinded? Maybe I am blinded, Lizzy. Come here. I'll have to do this by feel, won't I?"

He moved across the room faster than she thought him capable of, grasping her wrist just as she snatched up the skimmer off the draining board.

"Oh no you don't," he whispered, gripping tightly with his rough, horny hand. "You can drop that right now." He twisted her arm and she let go of the skimmer which clattered to the stone floor with an echoing clang.

"You're hurting me!" she said. "You'll break my wrist like that."

"Then stop struggling, eh?" He pulled her towards him and began to grope at her clothing. The freezing air between them boiled with their hot breath like the fog rolling in off the hills in the early morning.

Edgar lurched closer and trapped her against the draining board. "Now, now. Gently, there," he breathed in her ear as he once again pulled her clothing up and tried to force his hand between her legs. She was incensed. He was trying to gentle her into acquiescence as he would a spirited but unbroken horse. "Come on, Lizzy. Stir yourself."

Lizzy leaned in to him. Let him think he'd won. Then she bit down hard on his lip and screamed Roy's name as loudly as her lungs would let her.

"You bitch!" he said, dabbing his fingers on his lower lip and bringing them away bloody. "You'll pay for that. And I've told you, your precious Roy ain't coming. I've fixed him!"

Now

ON SATURDAY EVENING, Hannah began to make her preparations for the morning. She chopped up the dried prunes with scissors and added them to the vine fruits in a big bowl. The brandy and the juice and zest of the lemon went over them, and she stored the covered bowl in the pantry.

"It's worth chopping up the nuts this evening as well," her gran said. "It means you can mix it all up in the morning. It's not a long job, I find, as long as you've got all your ingredients to hand."

Hannah went down to the kitchen early on Sunday, before anyone but her father was moving. He'd been out before first light and into the milking parlour. It was freezing cold in the kitchen. She went over to the radiator and put her hand on it. Surprisingly, it was hot but the air, even just above it, was chilly. "Weird," she said, with a puff of vapour.

She put her hand on the long worktop ready to reach into the cupboard below it, and pulled it sharply back. The dark grey granite was icy. In fact, she was able to trace frosty fern-fronds, scraping them off with her fingernail. This was ridiculous. She'd have to ask Dad to get the plumber or the heating engineer in. Although it was a sharp, end-of-November morning, it shouldn't be this cold in here.

Hannah retreated into the front hall to grab her fleece jacket. It must warm up in the kitchen soon, especially once she started cooking. Suitably togged up, she got out the steamer and the big stew-pan which she made into an improvised second steamer by putting an upturned saucer inside it. Once the water was on to boil, she took out the big old bread pancheon her mum still used and started to measure out the ingredients into it. Yesterday her gran had told her that the worktop on the outside wall of the kitchen was where she'd felt the chill and heard the voice. That's exactly where Hannah had just wiped off the frost. Ridiculous. She wasn't going to fall for all the superstition stuff. There was a glitch in the central heating system, that was all.

Taking the soaking fruit from the pantry, she put it into the massive stoneware bowl with the other ingredients as directed in the old family recipe book. The book almost fell open at this page, with eggy smears and little greasy marks over the yellowing paper. Every so often, she paused to blow on her hands. Manipulating the biggest of her mother's wooden spoons through this mixture was hard work, even when your hands were warm enough to get a good grip. It wasn't long before she could hear her mother moving about in the bathroom directly upstairs. She left the spoon in the bowl and crossed the room to where the big baking dishes were kept. Pulling out two huge, deep pudding basins, she greased them with a bit of butter then set about cutting greaseproof paper to cover them.

"Hello, love," her mum said. "I see you've got on well. Must be nearly time for me to have my three stirs?"

"I think so," Hannah said, turning back to the granite work surface where the wooden spoon lay next to the pancheon, some of its sticky mixture dripping onto the surface.

"Don't leave it like that, Hannah," her mum said. "You're wasting the mixture."

"I didn't, Mum," she said. "I left it in the bowl."

"Well you can't have done, can you? Or it would still be in there. I'm going to open a window or two in here to let the steam out. They're going to be running with water soon, it's so hot in here."

Hannah walked over to her mum and put her hands on her mother's cheeks.

"Oh, Hannah, you're freezing! Have you been outside? How in heaven's name did you get that cold?"

"I'm not sure heaven has much to do with it, Mum."

Then

LIZZY WAS SHOCKED at her own temerity. She'd bitten Edgar's lip, hard. He stepped back, dabbing at his face with a filthy kerchief and bringing it away with bloodstains.

"You'll regret that, you little madam. I'll be back!'

She leant back against the stone sink, her heart thumping and her chest heaving for breath. She watched him slink out again, still wincing but casting her that evil, sly look. Had she just put off the inevitable?

Moments later there was a commotion from somewhere across the yard. Fly, the farm dog, set up such a barking and a clamour that she wondered if the house was on fire. She knew her duty was in the dairy but she had to see what had upset Fly. She was a good dog and it was difficult to rattle her like this.

Lizzy found herself hoping Fly was trying to see Edgar off the premises. Serve him right, too!

The dog put her head round the dairy door, just for a moment, then, still barking, ran across the yard again. Lizzy followed. Something was wrong. The dog was dancing about, running to the milking shed, then back to Lizzy as though wanting her to follow.

She gathered up her skirts and followed the dog. Was it Roy? She screwed her eyes to see into the gloom. Her hands flew to her face.

"Roy? Oh, Lord above, Roy!" The cowman lay as still as death. She ran over to him, the dog still barking and leaping around her.

"Fly! Lie down!" The dog dropped as though shot.

Farmer came in after her. He flung the door wide to let in more light. Roy had been hit on the back of the head with a huge billet of wood.

"Look at this," Farmer said, holding the wood up. It had hair and blood sticking to the end. Lizzy felt Roy's head and saw his chest rising and falling. She also noted the unnatural angle of one of his legs.

"What's happened here?" the farmer asked, as

though she had anything to do with it.

"I bet anything it's that Edgar Burton," Lizzy sobbed. "He's been… he's been here pestering me all morning and when I said I'd shout for Roy, he told me he'd fixed him. Oh, what'll we do?"

Mrs Caldwell had joined them at this point, having heard Lizzy's cries and the dog's fussing. While she helped the girl to her feet and led her away over the muddy yard, the farmer and Billy lifted Roy into the cart to take him home to his mother.

"Calm down, Lizzy, for heaven's sake, and tell me what happened there."

"It was that Edgar, Missus." Lizzy's eyes still streamed as she spoke.

"Edgar Burton? What was he doing here today?"

"He come to… make a nuisance of himself. You know? He wanted to… make free wi' me. And I wouldn't have none of it. He's been in here twice this morning and the last time, not many minutes since, I bit him to make him leave off. And… and if that Edgar sees me again, I think he'll kill me. I fought him off, see, and I made him bleed. I spoiled his sneerin' smilin' face. You oughter seen the mad look in his eye when I done that."

"Come into the kitchen, Lizzy. I'll make you some tea. Let's get you warmed up or Edgar won't need to kill you. You'll get your death of cold."

Now

GRAN CAME IN and caught the looks on the faces of Hannah and her mother. "What's up, girls?" she asked. It amused Hannah to hear her mum being called a girl, but to Grandma Clark, Mum was the girl who'd married her son. "Shall I put a pot of coffee on?"

"That'd be grand," said Mum. "Our Hannah's had a bit of a fright, haven't you, love?"

"She wasn't over there?" asked her gran, nodding at the bowl and spoon on the long worktop.

"Yes. It was a bit creepy, that's all."

"Did you feel cold?"

For an answer, Hannah held her fingers to her grandmother's face, as she had to her mother's. Old Mrs Clark took the hands in her own to warm them up. "Let's get some hot coffee down you and then you can tell me all about it."

"Someone say coffee? I don't suppose there's any breakfast on the go?" Liam bounced into the room like a puppy and looked from face to face. "What?" he asked, seeing their expressions.

His mother told him that the top of the cooker was in use for the steamers but he could have a bacon roll if he put some under the grill. "You might as well do enough for us all," she said. "Your dad will be in soon and our Hannah's had a bit of a shock."

By the time her father came in from the milking, rubbing his hands together and blowing a nose reddened by the wind, Hannah had put the Christmas pudding mixture into the bowls, greased and pleated the paper for the lids and tied them on with string. Her gran showed her how to make the string into a handle which crossed the bowl from side to side so it could be lifted out of the pan when it was done.

"Right," said her mum, rubbing her hands together. "That's it for another year."

Everyone sat around the table and took a bacon sandwich, and quiet fell upon the group for a few minutes. "What was up with everyone when I came in?" asked Liam. "It looked like a wet Whit Week in here. As my gran would say." He smiled at his gran and shoved the last bite into his mouth.

Hannah said, "Just had a creepy feeling when I was mixing the puddings, that's all."

"Someone walk over your grave?" asked their dad.

"I thought you said that when someone shuddered suddenly?" she asked. "I mean, I did shudder I suppose, but it was with cold. The temperature dropped. In fact when I came down earlier, there was frost on the granite worktop."

"Get on!" her dad said. "I must have been through here not half an hour before that and it was lovely and toasty."

"She'll be right about that, Geoff," said Gran. "I've felt it myself. But only on Stir-up Sunday."

"This is getting a bit weird for me," he said. "I've got fence posts to fix. I'll see you all later."

Liam pushed his chair back with the sort of loud scrape that earned him a scowl from his mum, and said he'd be back for dinner.

"I'll bet," his gran said. "When we've washed up I'll get the vegetables ready, shall I?" Hannah's gran stayed most weekends and loved to be involved once again in the life of the farm. She'd been here from her teenage years and this house was all she'd known, until she and Granddad bought the bungalow when he was eventually persuaded to retire.

There wasn't much to do after that but Hannah couldn't leave the house. She'd set the timer for two hours and would need to top up the steamers. She took a cloth over to the worktop to wipe up the dripped mixture. She knew she'd left the spoon in the bowl. She wasn't losing it that badly. The worktop was once again icy cold. Getting a grip on her fears, she reminded herself that the whole purpose of a granite slab was that it was cold. All the better for pastry making. It wasn't usually this cold, though. Was it?

With both hands on the surface, she closed her eyes. The slab was so icy! The air was so whispery and strange. It must be the blood rushing to her head, or her ears whooshing with the sound of her heartbeat. She felt a little giddy and had to steady herself. From out of the air, from the midst of the whispering words, she picked out something she felt must be aimed at her.

"Lizzy. Come on, girl. Stir yourself."

The whisper, on the cusp of hearing, created a tiny, ice-cold draught against her ear – but had she heard that or had she just imagined it? Lizzy? That was her middle name but nobody called her that. Did they?

Then

LATER THAT MORNING, Mrs Caldwell put her arms around Lizzy. "Don't worry, dear. My husband won't have Edgar Burton back here, not if he treats you like that. And if he so much as catches sight of him round here again, he'll have the law on him for the way he's assaulted our stockman. That man's been a heap of trouble and he's getting worse."

"But poor Mrs Samuels. Roy won't be able to work for weeks, maybe a couple of months, with a broken leg. What'll they do?" Lizzy broke into fresh tears at the thought.

"Lizzy! You don't think we'll let a good stockman starve, do you? We can't afford his wages, not with having to get someone else in to do the milking, but we can make sure the Samuels have a hot meal every day. That Edgar Burton owes us for this. It was just a jealous rage from the sound of it."

Lizzy pulled herself together in the knowledge that Roy and his mother would have food on the table while his leg and his head mended.

"Now you get a hold of yourself, Lizzy. As soon as we get Fred to finish the milking, there'll be work for you here. It may be the day we make the Christmas puddings but that doesn't mean everything else has to stop, does it?"

"No, Missus. Sorry." She blew her red nose again, wiped her still-streaming eyes and tugged at her dishevelled costume.

"And for goodness' sake, go and get a wash and put your other dress on, will you?"

Pudding day was an exciting one with its exotic smells and its promise of Christmas treats to come, but as Mrs Caldwell had said, in every other respect it was a working day. The poor cows couldn't cross their legs till morning so she must get on with the work. Most days Farmer would take the churns round the village with his measuring can and people would come out to buy their milk, carrying it back in a jug from their own kitchen. But first, Lizzy had to let the rich milk settle and skim the cream off. She had the churn to wind and wind. What a tiring job that was, waiting for the butter to turn. Throw a bit of salt in and then skim the golden butter off the buttermilk. Farmer sometimes sold that, too, but often Mrs Caldwell would use it in the baking. It helped her to make her prize-winning scones.

By the end of a working day, she was exhausted. Nobody stayed up late on the farm. Their working day began so much earlier than most folks'.

Now

"SEEN A GHOST, GIRL?" Hannah's dad asked when he called in at midday for a snack.

"No, but I think I might have heard one," Hannah said. She still felt shaky.

"Rubbish! No such thing," he stated as he ate scrambled eggs and toast.

"That's what I used to think," said her gran.

"Oh, come on now, Mum. You're not encouraging her in this nonsense, are you?"

"Whooo! Ghosties!" cried Liam, breaking out into the X-Files tune.

"The truth is in there," said Hannah, knocking on his head with her knuckle.

Dad put his fork down, pushed his chair back and said, "Right, out with it. What's all this about?"

Hannah told him what she'd felt, and more recently heard, and was pleased to have her gran

41

backing her up.

"Why have you never mentioned this before, Mother?" he asked.

"Because I knew I'd get this reaction, that's why. You're scoffing at your daughter and you'd have scoffed at your mother too. And nobody else had ever felt it before, except me. Not till our Hannah said she'd felt the frost in here this morning. Then I knew it was still happening. I didn't want to sound like a mad woman." She shot a harsh look at Liam when he began to snigger.

"What about you, Mum?" Hannah asked. "Did you ever get a strange feeling over at the old dairy side of the kitchen?"

"Can't say I have, love. Mind you, I'm not what you'd call sensitive."

Liam continued to snigger.

Hannah added, "And funnily enough, the voice said, 'Stir yourself, Lizzy,' or something like that. The way Gran says, 'Shape yourself,' when we're messing around and she wants us to get on with something. And my middle name's Lizzy. Well, Elizabeth at any rate."

"Well, mine isn't and I've heard it too," said her gran.

"I remember now. You weren't that keen on us calling her Hannah Elizabeth, were you?" said Dad. "Is this why?"

Gran looked down at the tablecloth, then looked back up, catching Hannah's eye. "It's not really that simple. But I've felt the unease in this kitchen, just as I did in the dairy back in the old days but now it's the same place, isn't it? It was always an uncomfortable place to hang around, the old dairy. I used to feel oppressed in there and sometimes I swore the shadows moved. You can laugh, our Liam," she added, scowling at her grandson, "but it's true. Something happened here, years ago, but we don't know what."

"Gran?" asked Hannah.

"Yes, love."

"Did you only hear the voice that once?"

"Yes. I never strayed over to that side of the kitchen again. Not on Stir-up Sunday, at any rate."

"You know when you heard that whispering?"

"Yes..." Her gran sounded hesitant.

"Could you feel anything? Anything like a cold draught?"

"I could indeed. It felt like a very icy breath was whispering the words right into my ear. I put my hands up to feel my face. I thought I'd find frost on my neck."

"Did you hear any other words? Anything else you could pick out?"

"Actually, yes. But not anything I could make sense of. I heard 'Lizzy' and 'stir' very plainly. The rest was like that shushing sound you get when you kick up autumn leaves. Indistinct. But… I dunno, it sounds daft if I say it out loud, but I thought it said 'pig pie'."

Liam roared with laughter, and banged his hand on the table for emphasis. "That ghost of yours must have lived here yonks ago, Gran. We call them pork pies these days, don't we? That reminds me, I wonder how long dinner will be. I'm starving!"

"You're always starving, dear."

"Well… Funny that, but I thought it said 'pigsty'," Hannah said.

"But we don't have a pigsty," Liam replied.

"There certainly was one, once," his gran said. "We had one here that I remember, and it was in use in my in-laws' generation. It was made of wood and roofed with corrugated iron, though, and it didn't last. Then, of course, it stopped being economical to keep a few pigs because you couldn't feed them scraps any more. That's more or less what people kept them for, you know. Garbage disposal. Well, pigsty makes more sense than pig pie, anyway!"

Now

Christmas Day

PRESENTS HAD BEEN OPENED, the vegetables prepared, the turkey was in the oven and the famous pudding was having its final steaming. Dad came in from the milking, his glasses fogging over from the heat of the room. The work had to be done, holiday or not.

"Ah, I can smell turkey," he said. "And pudding! That reminds me – is anyone bored? What do you say we kill a couple of hours checking the farm's journals for Lizzy? Queen of Puddings!"

"Do they go back very far?" asked Liam, beginning to look interested.

"They do – and I still keep one," said Dad. "It's a good way of recording temperatures, weather conditions, crop yields, sowing dates and all the rest.

Back when they had a lot of men to run the farm, their names and occupations were recorded too. Like when they were taken on, when they left, and such. These days it's usually only a one- or two-man operation, a farm this size. There's no need for that kind of information. Mine's mainly weather and crop yields."

"How old's the farm, Gran?" Hannah asked.

"I should think this land's been farmed for thousands of years, love. But this house was built in the 1700s and we've got some sort of records all the way back. They'll be in your dad's office. Unless he's thrown them out, of course."

"I wouldn't do that!" Dad was adamant. "This farm is in my blood. I couldn't chuck out anything that's related to its past."

"We ought to look!" Hannah bubbled and shifted on her chair.

She, Liam and their grandmother followed Dad into the farm office where the journals were kept. "Blimey, there's loads of them!" Liam said.

"There's one for each year," Gran said, "so there are bound to be lots. Your dad bundled them up into tens with string, so at least we can take a ten-year block and go through them. Are you sure you want to do this?"

"Yeah, why not?"

"Well, I thought you might feel it was a waste of a Christmas morning, that's all."

"Can we bring them through to the kitchen?" Hannah asked. "Because I've got to keep my eye on the steamer so it doesn't boil dry. Seeing as I'm the one who heard the voice – oh, and Gran, of course – I think I should be able to help with this."

Liam nodded. "Yeah, the more of us who go through these, the quicker we'll find what we're looking for."

"What do you think we actually *are* looking for, Liam?" asked their gran.

"No idea," he said with a wide grin, "but I'll know it when I see it!"

"The confidence of youth," said Hannah with a sigh. She had no idea why her gran laughed.

They carried a few bundles each back to the big kitchen table and began to unpack them. "Only untie one bundle each at a time," Hannah suggested. "We don't want to mix them up and have to start sorting them out again."

"Well, I would never have thought of that," said Liam.

"You are so unfunny when you're being sarcastic."

Gran snapped, "Look, you two. If we're going to get anywhere with this we need to do it and not waste time sniping at one another."

Hannah looked up quickly. It was unusual for her gran to be so tetchy. She wasn't the only one on edge about this.

They settled into the task and Liam's excitement was contagious. The job was slowed down by the need they all felt to read out bits of the journals to one another.

"This would make a brilliant book," said Hannah.

"It'd be a bit dry," her gran said. "It's just dates and facts and the like."

At a sudden beeping sound, Hannah leapt up and re-boiled the kettle to top up the steamer. "Anyone for a hot drink while I'm up?"

It was Gran who pointed out that it might be better to wait. "We don't want coffee stains on these books. They're an amazing record and they're irreplaceable."

"I've found an Elizabeth – here in 1723. She was the farmer's daughter."

"Put a bookmark in that page. Keep looking." Gran was confident that the first Elizabeth wasn't necessarily the answer. "I think Elizabeth was a common name in those days."

Liam seemed to go off the boil now the hard work had begun. He spent the next fifteen minutes reading out what he felt to be comic names. "Here, listen to this – Obediah. Do you reckon his mum called him Obi? Hey! Maybe that's what Obi-Wan Kenobi's name really was? Obediah. Poor devil!"

"Liam! Are you doing this or not?" his sister chided.

Finally, Liam struck gold. "Here's a Lizzy! She's not given as Elizabeth, either. Lizzy Pelham, dairymaid."

"That's got to be her!" cried Hannah. Her face flushed. "It's all connected with the old dairy, isn't it,

Gran? When was that?"

"1783. It says, 'Taken on new dairymaid. Lizzy Pelham, aged 13.'"

They traced mention of Lizzy through the following three or four years. Naturally, with all the farm records in there, and the names of all the other staff when they came or went, she didn't get much of a mention. A couple of years later she was recorded as helping Mrs Caldwell with the Christmas puddings.

"Look! 'Stir-up Sunday. My wife and Lizzy made puddings.' That's our link. Keep looking." Hannah found herself almost sick with excitement. "Do you think it's Lizzy's ghost?" she asked.

"Can't be, can it?" said Gran. "Why would it talk to itself? Why would it be speaking to Lizzy?"

"It could be. Hannah talks to herself," Liam said. "Ow, Gran. Tell her. She kicked me!"

Finally, Dad suggested that they stick to looking at that date each year. "If she's making the puddings, and Gran and Hannah got their spooky voices when they were making them too, let's see what happens on that day each year afterwards.

Where's the rest of the pile?"

Lizzy turned up in the following couple of years, making the puddings on her own. Again, it was Liam who found the telling reference.

"Hey! Listen to this. In 1787 – that's when she's seventeen – it's got this. 'Stir-up Sunday and what a dark day for the farm. All started well, Lizzy making the Christmas puddings and my wife boiling them as always. I was later drawn to the yard by the wild barking of Fly, my dog, and the screaming of Lizzy. My stockman, Roy, found half out of his senses, badly beaten, his leg broken. He will not work for many weeks. Lizzy told us of the farrier being here, which he was not due to be till next week. He tried to force himself upon her and attacked Roy. This is not the worst of it. By evening, Lizzy herself had disappeared. We can find no trace of her and will have to send word to her parents' home to see if she is gone back there.'"

"Good heavens!" said Mum. "To think of goings-on like that here on our farm."

"I'm going to keep going through the next year or so," Liam said. "I have to find out what happened. Did she come back? Is she a 'misper'?"

Hannah laughed. "You watch too many detective programmes!"

Liam found that the stockman was a Roy Samuels and the farrier was Edgar Burton. He also found that there was never any further trace of Lizzy Pelham. She never returned to the farm. Just before Christmas 1787 came the entry, 'Engaged the services of Isaac Wilson, farrier, Burton having disappeared when Lizzy did.'

"That seems to be that, then," said Hannah. "They both disappeared around the same time. Sinister, or what?"

"Hey!" Liam shot up in his seat. "I could go and look on the computer in the library?"

"What's wrong with the farm computer?" his dad asked.

"Nothing wrong with it – but we haven't got a subscription to Ancestry, have we? I'll try and find Edgar Burton and Lizzy Pelham. The Missing Links!"

Then

DUSK WAS FALLING. Though the dark came early at this time of year, it had been a long and a bad day's work here at Yew Tree Farm. It seemed sad, and somehow trivial, that people had been preparing for a Christmas which they would not all see.

Fighting over a woman was so old-fashioned. It wasn't the way the toffs did it. They indulged in the more stately duelling, but here nobody entered the fray with a second and a box of carefully tended pistols. Nobody counted to ten or dropped a satin handkerchief. It was more basic, this. Instinctive and brutal. When it came down to it, the instincts were animal. Fight, grab, take what you want. Still, that's how things are. Primitive urges – primal needs. And dead bodies.

The sun went down in a blaze of red and

turquoise. The figure stopped for a moment to look, but the spectacle didn't last more than a few minutes. The last of the brightness dropped from the afternoon and the dimmer, harder lights of stars and moon showed the way. Frost had once again descended and the rutted ground crunched underfoot. The going was rough. That made it so much harder to transport the burden.

Behind the figure, pulling it into a stooped position with the effort, was a dark shape. A bundle of sorts. From the difficulty involved in dragging it, it must have been heavy. At least the gathering frost made it possible to tug the bundle over the ruts without leaving a trail. There would be no telltale groove for anyone to follow. Nobody would know, come the morning.

The figure began to tire. It stopped to rest every so often. The jolting over the frozen ruts caused the bundle to begin to unwrap. Dropping the cloth at the end, the figure went round to re-wrap its burden. Standing again suddenly, it listened, but identified only the eerie scream of a vixen – lonesome, mournful and terrifyingly human. Apparently satisfied, it continued to retie its bundle then to tug it behind, towards the low, looming building close by.

Finally it dropped the ends of the cloth and stood to gaze at the disturbed ground to the side of the derelict building. The old pigsty. It had begun to deteriorate some years ago and had been replaced. Now it was even more ruinous. Ivy crept around it and strangled the last few stones in the low walls. There was a hole in the ground, dug surreptitiously earlier in the day while the soil was softer and now visible only as a darker shadow. All that was needed was to tip in the bundle, push the soil back over with the old spade which leant on the battered stonework, and tamp it down.

Easier said than done. The figure rested for a few moments, leaning against the crumbling stone of the pigsty wall, its breath cloudy before its hooded face. Gradually the breathing slowed and the figure stood to resume its self-imposed task. Roll the bundle, clamber in after it to straighten the rough wrappings, haul oneself out. Cover the buried treasure with the loose, frosty soil.

Done. As the figure stood to put one frozen hand

to its back for support, it looked up into the black sky above, where the ice-shard stars were now obscured as the first snowflakes of winter began to swirl in a keen wind. They glittered like gems and fell, unheeding, upon the work of this night, obscuring the disturbed soil and the rutted ground of the field, casting their gentle white blanket over all. Nature would provide a shroud. The figure, now visibly tired, shambled off into the night, leaning on the spade for support.

Now

Christmas Dinner

IT WAS A POIGNANT Christmas dinner; the last Hannah would have while living at home.

"Honestly, look at the long faces," Liam kept saying. "You'd think someone was dying!"

They sat around the big farmhouse kitchen table, leaning back in satisfaction after the roast turkey and all the traditional accompaniments.

"Anyone got room for pudding?" asked Mum.

"I'll say," said Dad. "Best bit of the Christmas dinner, that is. And this year, it's our Hannah's first attempt."

"Attempt? It's a damned good pudding, is that!" said the pudding-mixer in mock outrage.

"I'm dying to get onto Ancestry," Liam said. "The start of the farm here, if it's in the 1700s, is before the censuses, so we'd have to go looking at the births, marriages and deaths records. That doesn't give you who was living where in such a simple form as the census. It's going to take a while. I don't think the library opens until after the New Year, either."

"You've got Lizzy, and Burton, and that Roy Samuels fellow to look at," said Hannah, dishing up the rich, steamy pudding. "That should keep you occupied for a while."

"You haven't got homework to do over the Christmas holidays, have you?" his mum asked.

"You have to spoil even Christmas Day, don't you?" he moaned. "We did have, but I got mine out of the way as soon as we broke up."

Mum looked down, her voice quiet now. "I wonder if the mystery will ever be solved."

"I don't know. And what about the pigsty, or my pig pie?" asked Gran.

"Good point," said Hannah. "Have you got any ancient maps of this place, Dad? You know, things where old or abandoned buildings might be marked?"

"We've got some old sale deeds," said Dad, helping himself to custard. "Whenever we bought or sold a bit of land, there was always a plan drawn up. A bit like you have a plan of a house or flat when you buy it, I suppose. I could go back through those. They're all in the deed box in the office."

"Oh, can we look? Now?" The laid-back Liam was animated again.

"Not now," said his father. "Right now, I'm eating my Christmas pudding. And I don't want to rush it." He sounded adamant. "Maybe I can give the keys to my research assistant after dinner?"

"Oh, yes! Yes please!"

"When he's helped to wash up."

A little later, they all pored over the old maps and documents spread out across the dining table. "Look at this!" cried Liam. Hannah had rarely seen her brother so excited. "Look! On this map, the one where our family bought part of the farm from the Caldwell family, it says, 'sheep fold, disused' and 'pigsty, disused'. So there were some buildings on the farm that aren't here now."

"Why did we only buy a part of the farm?" she

asked.

"You'd have to ask your great-granddad about that, and he's not here any longer," said Dad. "Looking at the maps, he bought a big chunk of it. It looks like that area with the quarries was sold off separately. Who knows why? Maybe the original family ended up with no children to take over the farm. And perhaps people were being picky – a buyers' market. Anyway, you now have your pigsty. Everybody happy?" He said this with a big wink at his wife, who slapped him with the tea-towel.

"Oh, that was a fantastic lunch, Mum," said Hannah, letting her belt out a notch. "I really ought to walk that off. Fancy a ramble, anyone?"

"Oh, Dad, can we go and look at the place where that pigsty is marked?" asked Liam.

"I don't see why not. It's not far, just over West Field, but I can tell you there's no building there now. Come to think of it, though, there's a bit of a jumble of stones there in the corner."

"Oh, wow! Come on, let's go there first."

"So what d'you reckon, Liam? The Haunted Pigsty?" Hannah wobbled her fingers and hummed

Liam's favourite X-Files tune.

"You can go if you like," said their mum. "I think Gran and I will sit here and nurse the coffee pot for an hour or so till you're ready to come back."

Hannah, Liam and their dad put on warm coats and set off through the farm yard and out of the gate. The place marked on the map was two fields away from the farm buildings.

"I wouldn't have thought this was a particularly convenient place for a pigsty if they were feeding them scraps?" Hannah said. "You'd have to come marching out here in all weathers."

"You've never smelt pigs, have you, love?" Dad said with a smile. "Back then, farm labour was cheap. You could keep a bucket for your food scraps by the back door and a couple of times a day you'd send one of the farm lads over to feed them. Keep the pigs themselves by the back door and they'd stink the place out. And there'd be flies in summer, too."

They walked briskly with hands in pockets, and climbed the stile into the pigsty field. In the far corner, a tumble of stones lay almost obscured by ivy and tussocky grass. The patch of earth beside it was damp, trodden by the feet of the cattle.

"Is this it?" Liam asked.

"You sound disappointed," Dad said.

"Well, after all Hannah and Gran said, it just looks a bit 'meh'."

"I don't know what you expected, really. It's just that you and our Hannah were so keen to check it out. I've been going past it for years – you two must have done, too?"

He looked at Hannah for confirmation but she stood shivering, with her shoulders hunched. She tried to take a step forward and staggered slightly. Dad rushed to grab her and guided her to the low field wall, so she could sit down.

"What's up, love? You've gone white."

"She's nearly blue, Dad. I can hear her teeth chattering and she's all but got frost on her!"

Dad took off his own coat and put it round her shoulders. "Do you feel ill, love?"

It was a moment or two before Hannah could speak. "I... I heard the voice again. It was a bit faint and whispery but... I heard the word 'pigsty' again…" Her voice tailed off as she shuddered violently. "Dad! We have to dig. We've got to find out what's here."

"Liam, run home for a hot water bottle, would you? And a flask of coffee to warm Hannah up. She can't walk home in this state and I don't reckon I can carry her these days."

"Can I get a couple of spades too? While she's warming up, we can be digging."

"I don't think that's a priority now. Let's just get something warm into her."

"Dad… let him get a spade. We need to dig." Hannah was insistent and eventually, with a curt nod to Liam, her dad agreed.

He sat close to her, his arm around her shoulders. "You're shaking, love. Was it that voice again that's upset you?"

"Yes, Dad. It's scary. I feel like I'm not in control of my own life."

"You know I don't believe in this ghost stuff, but even I can see you're in shock. I wish that lad would hurry up!"

Minutes later, Hannah pointed a shaking hand

toward the farm buildings. "There he is. They've all come, look."

Liam carried two spades and his mum followed with the flask and hot water bottle. Even Gran had come along, clutching a blanket.

Mum and Gran sat on the wall on either side of Hannah, each with an arm around her as she sipped the hot drink. To calm her agitation, Dad and Liam set to with the spades in the place she indicated, though Liam needed no further incentive. They plunged them into the rich earth like a knife through cheese.

When she'd finished the coffee, a little colour returned to Hannah's cheeks and she began to take an interest. Only a short while later, Dad's spade made a sharp sound and he began to scrape it slowly over his discovery. "Bone," he said.

Hannah and her gran exchanged looks. "It's true then," Gran whispered.

Liam dropped his own spade and started scraping away the chilly earth with his hands. "There's more," he said, pulling at some dark shreds of fabric with trembling fingers. He sat back on his heels and his face drained of colour. Just for the moment, he looked shocked.

"Right, that's it, our Liam," his gran said. "Out you come. You could be messing about in a crime scene. I think we need the police out here, Geoff."

Now

Christmas Night

"WELL, I DIDN'T THINK we'd be finishing Christmas with a visit from the police!" said Hannah's mum.

"They said they won't be here till morning," Dad said. "The light's nearly gone now."

"It was horrible this afternoon," said Hannah. "Such a shock, actually seeing the bones there in the ground."

"It wasn't horrible. It was great!" Liam was full of it now that he'd recovered.

"Aye," his dad said. "That body can only have stayed undisturbed because the ground there's permanent pasture. If we'd ploughed it, it would have come up earlier. It was only fairly shallow, you know."

"I bet it's Lizzy Pelham," Liam said, his eyes sparkling. "I bet that Edgar bloke killed her because she wouldn't run away with him."

"You're so gruesome," said Hannah. "Let's wait and see."

"I'll find out eventually, when I can get to the library. I'll see if she really disappears. I'm going to look for her death date first of all. If she's not recorded with a date of death then he did her in!"

"Not necessarily," said Hannah. "She might have got married. Then she'd be recorded with her married name, wouldn't she?"

"Well, yeah. But then they'd put née Pelham, wouldn't they? If she's out there, I'll find her!"

After tea, Liam was annoying Hannah so much that she asked him what was wrong. "It's this mystery. The bones. You must admit, it's better than telly. D'you reckon Dad'd cough up for an Ancestry subscription?"

"No chance!" Hannah said. "Dairy farming's not that well-paid, you know."

"But... but aren't you dying to know what happened? I mean, can you really wait for the library to open again? I'm sure it's not till after New Year."

Hannah bit her lip. "How much is it? The subscription thing? Let's nip into Dad's office and look. I might – just might, mind you – be prepared to use my credit card."

With a whoop of delight, Liam rushed to switch on the computer. "Don't think you're getting your hands on the card," Hannah said. "If I decide I can afford it, you can go out of the room while I type in the number."

Liam searched for the Ancestry website and discovered it was possible to have a fourteen-day free trial. Dad heard his shriek from two rooms away.

Hannah soon became bored and wandered out of the room but Liam persisted. After much clicking and tutting, he seemed to have found what he was after. He called her back in. "Listen to this. It turns out that Lizzy simply disappears from our farm altogether. Next she's shown about six years later in a marriage record as Lizzy Pelham, spinster, working as a kitchen maid at Oldfield House in Gloucestershire and marrying Joseph Carpenter, bachelor, working as a gardener there."

"What about her death?" Hannah asked.

"Lizzy Carpenter's death is recorded in 1836. She was sixty-six years old then."

Liam's earlier proclamation that the bones they'd found – a complete human skeleton – were those of Lizzy Pelham, had proved incorrect.

The next day, Boxing Day, a team from the local police came to the farm mid-morning. After some discussion with Hannah's dad, they went out to the field and put a kind of tent around the area, much to Liam's disgust. "I can't see a thing!"

"They said it's Home Office regulations," his dad said. "If they're exhuming a body, they have to treat it with respect – which is more than you're doing."

"I am! I just want to see!"

"Well, when they've removed the bones for examination they'll let us know, I'm sure. They might even want a pathologist to look at them. Tell them if they're recent or if they've been there too long to follow it up as a crime."

Later, they heard back from the police. The bones were those of a man. According to the police doctor, they belonged to a tall man, strongly muscled, and in his early thirties. The back of his skull had been driven into his brain cavity by the blow which had been the cause of his death.

"Strongly muscled would fit a farrier, wouldn't it?" asked Hannah. "All that beating of horseshoes and stuff. He'd have arms on him like a weightlifter."

"He would, yes," her dad said. "Don't forget, though, that most men who worked on the land in those days would have had impressive muscles. It was just a more physical way of life, back then."

"So what about Edgar Burton?" Hannah asked. "Does he appear again anywhere or do you think he's our buried body?"

"I'll go and interrogate the Ancestry website again," said her brother. She could see that Liam was loving the mystery and the chase.

Eventually he reported back to the family. "Burton just falls off the face of the planet, as far as the records go. Like with Lizzy, I can find a birth record. Sometimes you can get a baptism record, and of course, if they do anything a bit off the rails or famous, there are the newspaper archives. You can get those at the library or online, too. But he's not there any longer. Oh, there are some Edgar Burtons that show up if you search, but not of the right age, going by his birth date."

"Looks like we found a name for our ghost, then," said Dad, looking first to his daughter, then his mother. "And it's looking increasingly as though our Lizzy is a killer."

"I'm a bit sad about that," Hannah said. "I felt sorry for her, with that Burton chap attacking her and all that. Now he's going to be properly buried, with a name on his grave, do you suppose that'll put a stop to the haunting?"

"I think we're going to have to wait to see how cold the kitchen is next Stir-up Sunday," said Gran.

Then

STILL SHAKING, though she couldn't have said whether it was more with fear or rage, Lizzy came back down to the dairy in her only other dress. Edgar had gone but she didn't believe he would let matters rest. She still had work to do, and began pouring the thick cream into the butter churn. She kept the big butter paddles, with the farm's mark – a yew tree – carved into them, close at hand. She didn't feel safe without some kind of weapon.

As she feared, when the afternoon was well on, the door swung open and Edgar Burton came in, his brow furrowed and his mouth downturned. His split lip looked reddened and sore, making his speech mumbled.

"There you are, Missy. Think you got away with it, do you? Come here!"

With that he made a lunge at her, but this time

Lizzy was ready. She grabbed up her butter paddle and swiped it at his face, aiming for the wound she had already inflicted.

He saw it coming, of course. Ducking and putting his arm up to protect his face, he took a step back. His foot caught in the supporting framework of the butter churn and, swinging his arms wildly in an attempt to prevent a fall, he toppled back onto the flagstones of the dairy floor.

Lizzy dropped her paddle and her hands flew to her face. If the sickening crack of bone on stone hadn't told her what she'd done, the gradually pooling blood beneath Edgar's head would have done so. She approached him slowly, fearing it was some kind of play-acting on his part, and that he would spring up again and grab her. He wasn't moving, though. He wasn't breathing. When she summoned the courage to put her finger on his neck, no telltale pulsing of blood showed him to be alive.

Fear spurred her on. She was sure Mrs Caldwell, knowing about the earlier attacks, would back her up, proclaiming her innocent. She was defending her honour. Surely a girl had that right? But she now knew she couldn't stay here. For her, this dairy would always be tainted by Edgar Burton's lust.

Still shaking with shock, she rushed to the little outhouse where the buckets, brushes and mops were stored, with which she kept her dairy clean. There were old sacks in there too, which she used to clean the floor of the rougher mud. Grabbing some sacking, she hurried back and, wincing at her own temerity, lifted Edgar's head and wrapped it in the coarse fabric to try to stem the tide of his seeping blood. It helped that it stopped her having to look at his face.

She lifted his feet and dragged him... the body... to the outhouse, managing to prop him in a sitting position in the corner. Lifting full churns of milk had made her strong. She returned with a bucket and mop, shuddering as she avoided the slick red trail glistening on her – no, no longer hers – *the* dairy flagstones. She had hated the man, true enough, but she hadn't envisaged this outcome.

Filling the bucket, she shaved a little hard soap into the water then dipped her mop in and stirred it about, to dissolve the soap. One... two... three. Three stirs and a wish! Did she regret that she'd spent hers on wishing Edgar Burton far away? Now he was as far as he could ever be.

She moved efficiently, though with more than the usual haste, and mopped away every trace of his blood. Stowing the cleaning materials back in the little shed, she turned her gaze away from the slumped figure in the corner, still ridiculously convinced that he would tug off the sack, wink and give her his nasty laugh if she looked at him. She still felt his dangerous presence in the dairy, though. Her mother always said she was too imaginative. Her mother! What would she do about her mother? She couldn't go home, now. They would look for her there. She could go to her cousin who worked in a big house in the next county. It would be a long walk of several days' duration but she'd given herself no alternative.

Hardly daring to breathe and with her heart still hammering, Lizzy returned to the churn, turning and turning until she felt the butter separate out. She began to make it into pats, hitting it furiously with the wooden paddles. She was angry with Edgar and with herself, though she didn't know what else she could have done.

The afternoons were short at this time of the year. When dusk began to hint at evening's approach, when everyone was busy finishing indoor jobs, Lizzy looked for the last time around the dairy. She had finished her tasks and left it all tidy as usual. No signs of any disturbance. Good.

While her hands had worked the butter, her mind had formed a plan. She took a spade from the barn and crossed the fields to the site of the old pig pen. It was tumbled down now, but there had always been a patch of damp ground beside it. Roy had told her there was a spring under there.

In thickening dusk, she dug a long trench, as deep as she could manage, then leant the spade by the tumble of stones as she put a hand to her back. It wasn't going to be so easy to drag a full-grown man over the grass to the makeshift grave. She had to get started, though, before she could begin a new life somewhere else.

Back at the farmyard, she slipped into the shed where she had to grope in the gathering gloom. She took as much sacking as she could find and, by feel, though it made her recoil in horror at times, she wrapped the icy cold body of Edgar Burton and tied a long end of the fabric to use as a hand-hold.

Only the stars and the shadowed moon saw her finally, close to exhaustion, push the farrier's body into his secret, unhallowed grave. No one would know. No one would mourn. She stamped the earth over him, patting it with the old spade, as the first snowflakes fell to cover the scene like a pall.

She had a long road ahead of her. Leaning on the spade, Lizzy Pelham left her old life behind and walked into her future.

Also by Kath Middleton:

Ravenfold

Message in a Bottle

Top Banana

Souls Disturbed

Beyond 100 Drabbles (with Jonathan Hill)

Is it Her? (with Jonathan Hill)

www.kathmiddletonbooks.com

Made in the USA
Charleston, SC
29 November 2016